MW00915766

Pumpkin Head Tom And Mummy Mary

PART I AND II

LENI, LIBBY, AND MIKE SCHRETTENBRUNNER

Copyright © 2021 Leni, Libby, and Mike Schrettenbrunner
All rights reserved
First Edition

Fulton Books, Inc.
Meadville, PA

Published by Fulton Books 2021

ISBN 978-1-64654-947-4 (paperback)
ISBN 978-1-64654-948-1 (digital)

Printed in the United States of America

Pumpkin Head Tom Meets Mummy Mary

When you look at Pumpkin Head Tom and Mummy Mary, you'd think they always had a very happy-go-lucky life... However, that wasn't always the case.

Sometimes things don't go as planned, and in the little town of Spooksville, sometimes witches have to make you. When Pumpkin Head Tom was made, he wasn't made correctly. Things kept falling.

Falling into a pot of witches' brew. They wanted an Apple Head Andy. Maybe they should have paid better attention to the ingredients.

When Mummy Mary was made, she was made by humans. They made Mary correctly. She is a Mummy. They made sure to use a lot of toilet paper.

Poor Tom was bullied at school because he wasn't made right. He's supposed to be an Apple Head, but he's a Pumpkin head, of course.

Mean children always shouted things like, "Apple Head Andy, yeah right!" and "You are supposed to be an apple!"

He was sad, sad, sad. But one day a bully yelled, "Your name should be Pumpkin Head Tom!" Then someone stood up for him. Do you know who it was...?

It was Mary!

They were friends from that day forward for years and years. Until one day...

They got married!

The End

Pumpkin Head Tom
and
Mummy Mary

Part II

After they got married, Tom and Mary bought their first home in Spooksville.

On their move-in day, they met their new neighbors, Frank and Frankie Stein.

Frank and Frankie have five children. Two girls and how many boys...?

Two + three = five.

They are very cute children.

Tom loves to play with Frank and Frankie's kids, but Mary can't. Do you know why?

That's right—Mary was pregnant, so she had to be careful. Mary felt like it took a long, long, lonnng time to see her babies.

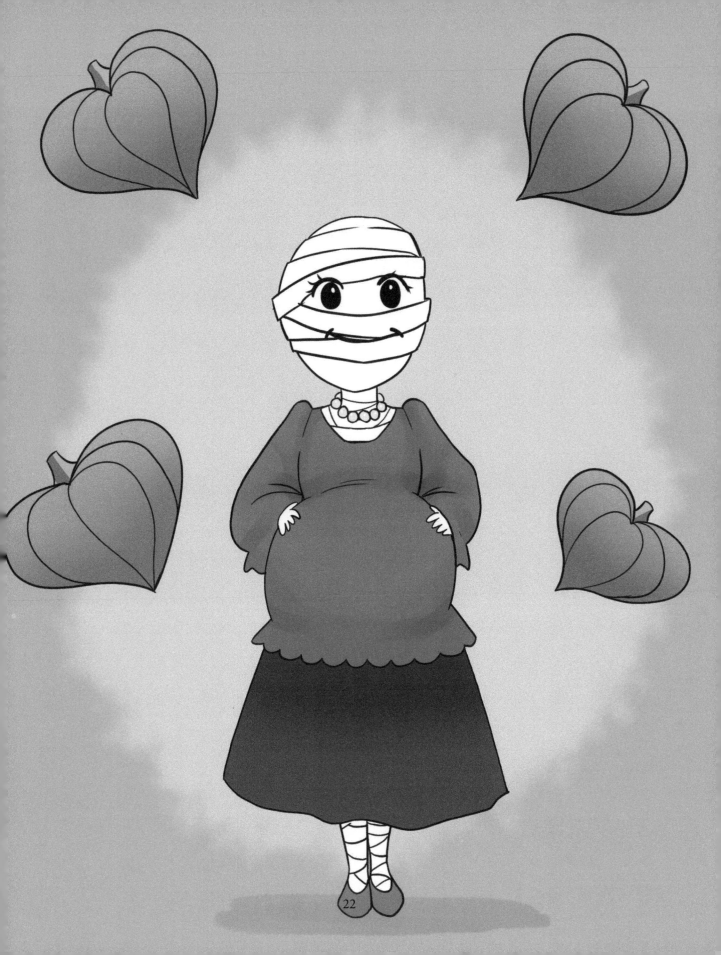

The days were long...

And the nights were even longer.

Then one day at work, Tom's boss Werewolf Walker told him to hurry home. Today is the big day.

When he got home, he was surprised to see, not one, but two Monster babies. He loved them at first sight. Do you?

ABOUT THE AUTHOR

I do not think it is uncommon for fathers to have difficulties finding fun activities to do with their daughters. I have a great relationship with my daughters, but still, I admit that most of the time, their mom gets top billing. A couple of years ago, myself and my two daughters sat down at a table together to create stories using our collective imaginations. This fun activity gave birth to our beloved characters Pumpkin Head Tom and Mummy Mary. After the first story was finished, Libby shared it with her classmates, and in turn, they asked for more, and more. The rest is history.

Leni is the first of three authors. Leni is in sixth grade. She is a Girl Scout. She enjoys playing her French horn, drawing, acting, playing with friends, and her Goldendoodle named Gertrude.

Libby is the second of three authors. Libby is in third grade. She is a member of the Brownies. She enjoys playing piano, dance, acting, and drawing. Libby says her awesome kindergarten teacher, Mrs. Spence, inspired her to be an author when she introduced her to "Elephant and Piggy" by Mo Willems.

Mike Schrettenbrunner is the third of three authors. He graduated as a member of Alpha Chi Honor Scholarship Society at George Mason University in 1999 with a bachelor's degree in marketing. He enjoys working with his clients in technology and AV Sales. He loves every minute he spends with his beautiful wife, daughters, and pup in the scenic Tri-City area, which encompasses Geneva, Batavia, and St. Charles, Illinois.

CPSIA information can be obtained
at www.ICGtesting.com
Printed in the USA
LVHW070657080521
686861LV00015B/632